THE AMAZING VOYAGE OF JACKIE GRACE

by Matt Faulkner

SCHOLASTIC INC.

New York Toronto London Auckland Sydney

Created with love for Amy

ISBN 0-590-44860-9

Copyright © 1987 by Matt Faulkner.
All rights reserved. Published by Scholastic Inc.
BLUE RIBBON is a registered trademark of Scholastic Inc.

12 11 10 9 8 7 6 5 4 3 2   5   1 2 3 4 5 6/9

Printed in the U.S.A.   08

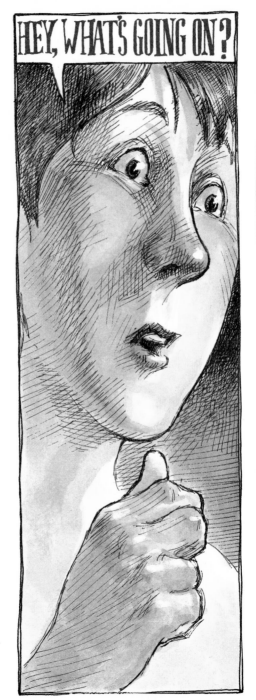

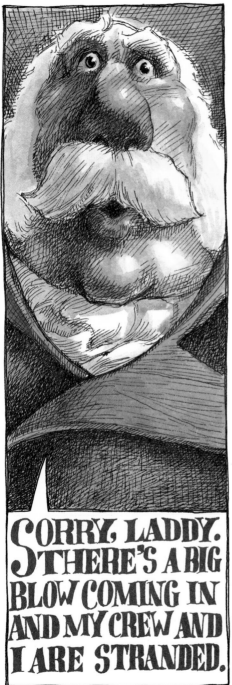

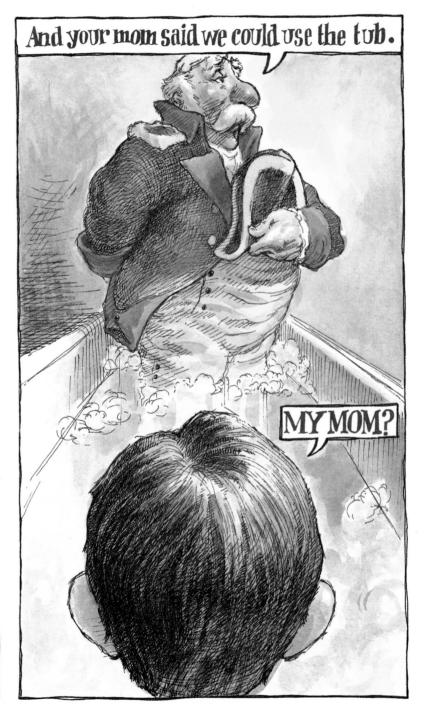

RIG UP A SAIL!

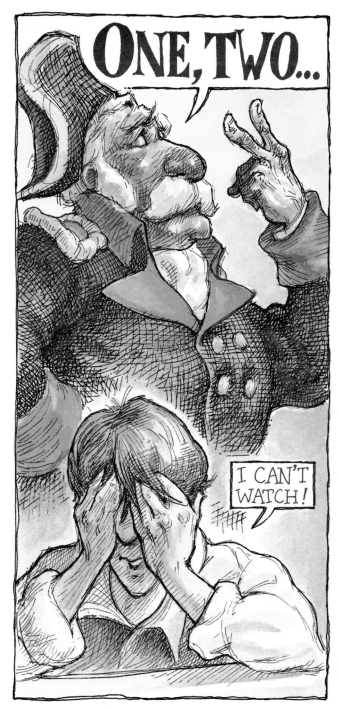

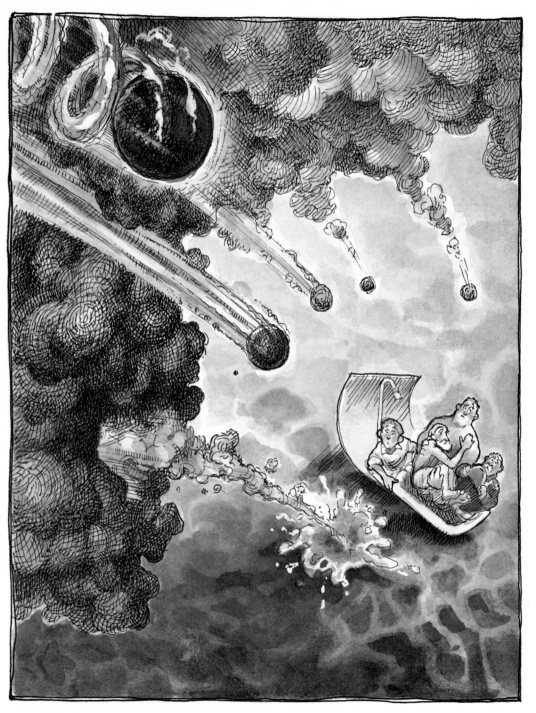

FIRE AT WILL!

WELL HELLO, RUNT. WELCOME ABOARD! HA!

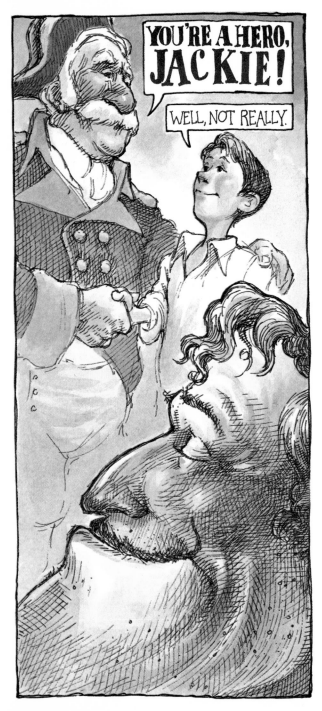

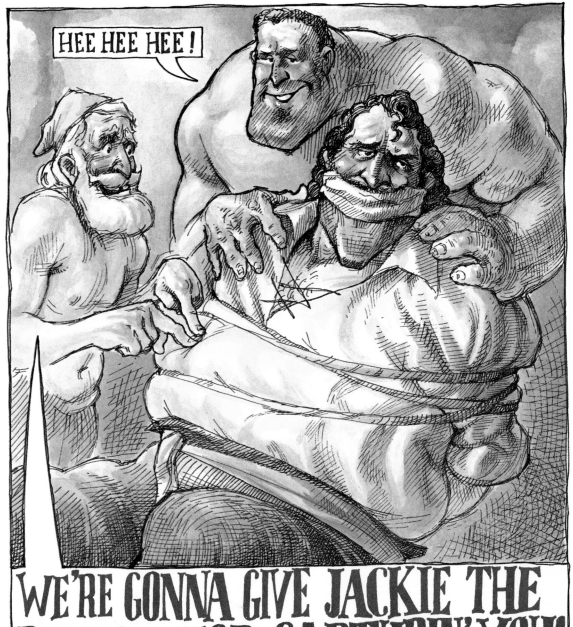